Victori?

Super ... to the Rescue

by Janey Louise Jones

illustrated by Jennie Poh

Capstone Young Readers
a capstone imprint

Superfairies is published by Capstone Young Readers
A Capstone Imprint
1710 Roe Crest Drive
North Mankato, Minnesota 56003
www.mycapstone.com

Text © 2018 Janey Louise Jones
Illustrations © 2018 Jennie Poh

Library of Congress Cataloging-in-Publication Data is available on the Library of Congress website.

ISBN: 978-1-62370-990-7 (paperback)
ISBN: 978-1-62370-991-4 (reflowable epub)

Summary: If the animals of Peaseblossom Woods are in trouble, it's up to the Superfairies to save the day! Rose, Berry, Star, and Silk keep their animal friends safe in these stories full of fairy power and friendship.

Designed by Tracy McCabe
Production specialist: Tori Abraham

For Anna
— Janey

For my husband, Jake,
and our two little fairies,
Aurelia and Evangeline
x — Jennie Poh

Printed and bound in the United States.

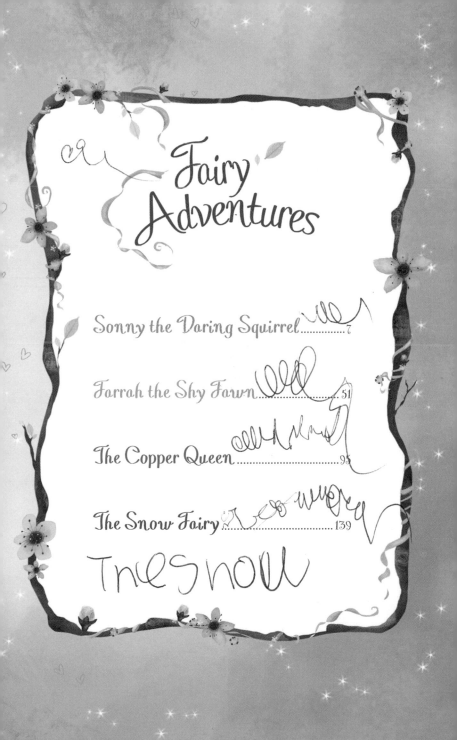

Fairy Adventures

TheSnow

The Fairy World

The Superfairies of Peaseblossom Woods use teamwork to rescue animals in trouble. They bring together their special superskills, petal power, and lots of love.

Superfairy Rose

can blow super healing fairy kisses to make the animals in Peaseblossom Woods feel better.

Superfairy Berry
can see for miles
around with her
super eyesight.

Superfairy Star
can create super dazzling
brightness in one dainty spin
to lighten up dark places.

Superfairy Silk
spins super strong webs
for animal rescues.

Superfairies

Sonny the Daring Squirrel

Table of Contents

Chapter 1

Wake Up to Springtime

Pink blossoms bloomed on the cherry blossom tree, which meant it was time for Duchess Tulip to visit the Superfairies in Peaseblossom Woods.

The four Superfairies were getting ready for her visit and a busy time ahead. The animals of Peaseblossom Woods were waking up after a long winter sleep. There would be more rescues for sure!

The four Superfairies — Rose, Berry, Star, and Silk — were looking at their springtime dresses in their wardrobes.

"We don't need our cozy winter clothes anymore!" said Star with a twirl. "I can't wait to wear my petal dresses without a cape! Spring clothes are so pretty!"

Silk spotted a curious-looking box next to the spring shoes.

"I wonder what's in that?" she said, fluttering toward it and taking off the lid.

"Oh! Look at this scrapbook I made about Duchess Tulip's last visit," she said, taking a petal-covered book from the box.

Rose, Berry, and Star gathered around to see the pictures sketched by Silk. There were scraps of twigs, leaves, and blossom petals saved from the last visit.

"Ooh, I love it when Duchess Tulip comes!" said Star. "She always brings sunshine and gentle breezes with her. And a few showers, of course!"

"We must make elderflower tea and rosehip honeybuns!" said Berry. "She loves those!"

"Yes," said Rose, "and we'll do the maypole dance with her as usual. That's always so fun. Oh, that reminds me — we should decorate the maypole."

"Where are the ribbons?" asked Silk.

"In our spring cabinet," said Rose, fluttering over to find them.

"Tada!" said Rose, finding the ribbons in spring colors — yellow, pink, blue, and green.

The four Superfairies flew outside and attached colorful ribbons to the maypole.

In the heart of the woods, on Lavender Lane, the little animals were delighted to be wide awake after the long, quiet winter rest. The young friends danced through the woods, singing silly songs as they went.

Sonny Squirrel was the youngest of all the animals, and he was all alone.

His mother had sent him out to collect twigs because he'd been pestering her to get outside.

"Don't go where you can't see our house!" his mother had warned.

But Sonny wandered farther through the woods, noticing the others having fun.

"Hey, can I join in?" he called.

"No, your legs are too short to keep up with us!" Basil Bear said with a laugh.

"Yeah, you're just a *baby*," said Billy Badger.

Sonny's sister, Susie, looked a little worried about him, but she didn't want to make a fuss in case the others laughed.

"I am not a baby!" said Sonny angrily.

"Prove it, then!" said Basil Bear.

Chapter 2

Sonny Shows Off

"Well," said Sonny, thinking hard.

"Yes?" said Basil with a smirk on his face.

"You see that log over there?" said Sonny.

"What about it?" said Billy Badger.

"I could jump off that!" said Sonny.

"Try it, then!" said Billy.

Sonny ran over to the log and flung himself onto it.

The other animals giggled because he looked so funny, trying to scramble onto the top of the log.

Once he was standing on it, he counted
to three and . . .

Jump!

He landed on the woodland floor.

"Told you I could!" said Sonny with
a wide grin.

"Anyone could do that!" said Basil.

"Leave him alone," said Martha Mouse. "He's just a baby."

"I AM NOT A BABY!" cried Sonny.

He was going to have to work harder to get the respect of the big boys.

Sonny looked around for ideas.

"You see the first branch of the tree up there?" he said, looking up at the lowest branch of a big oak tree. "I could jump from that!"

"I'd like to see you try!" said Basil.

Little Sonny darted up the tree trunk to the first branch. He crawled along it on his tummy. *Oh no, it's a long way down from here*, he thought. *Why did I say I'd jump?*

Poor little Sonny gathered all his courage and one, two, three . . .

Jump!

He was scared as he fell, but he didn't show it.

Phew, I made it, he thought as he landed on the ground with a thud.

"Anyone could jump from the first branch," said Basil with a snicker.

"Yeah, we did that when we were much younger than you!" said Billy.

Sonny was so disappointed that the older boys did not admire him like he had hoped. Instead of giving in, he tried to think of a more impressive stunt that he could do.

"I can climb to the very top of the tree and jump off! I won't even get scared! I've done it lots of times," boasted Sonny, who was telling lies now.

"Go ahead, then," said Basil. "I'd like to see this."

"No, Sonny!" cried Susie. "You will get hurt, and Mom and Dad will be angry with you. Plus, I will get in tons of trouble for not stopping you!"

"Well, don't watch," said Sonny. "Then you can't be blamed for not stopping me!"

Susie and Martha went down to the riverbank. They couldn't bear to watch Sonny trying to impress Basil and Billy.

"The thing is," said Martha. "Even if they were impressed, they'd never admit it, so Sonny is wasting his time."

"Exactly," agreed Susie. "I'm very annoyed with Basil and Billy!"

Back at Lavender Lane, Sonny bravely started to make his way up the trunk of the huge tree. His little heart thumped in his chest as he clambered to the top.

He slipped . . . but he held on. Up and up and up he went.

As he got higher and higher, Sonny felt dizzier and dizzier.

Oh no! he thought. *Why did I say that I've done this lots of times? I've never even done it once before. I'm very scared.*

Once he was on a very high branch, the woodland floor looked like such a long way down. It was too far to jump.

What will I do? he thought.

"Go, Sonny!" cried Billy.

Susie and Martha could hear what was going on. They made their way back to see Sonny.

Sonny began to feel dizzy with fear as he swung back and forth. He clung on to the branch.

Everyone could see that it was too high.

"Don't do it!" cried Susie.

"Come down, Sonny!" called Basil from below. "You will hurt yourself if you jump."

But Sonny didn't want to fail. He closed his eyes and tiptoed along to the tip of the branch.

If I scramble down now, they will think I'm a coward. They will never let me play with them, Sonny thought.

So he stepped off the branch into midair.

"Aaarggghh!" cried Sonny as he hurtled toward the ground, doing somersaults as he went.

"No!" sobbed Susie.

"Oh, Sonny!" cried Basil and Billy, feeling very worried and guilty.

The four friends felt helpless as they watched Sonny fall.

Chapter 3

Duchess Tulip Saves the Day

Duchess Tulip flew through the woods carrying gifts for the Superfairies. She flew so fast that if you blinked, you'd miss her. But she brought with her the air of spring, and the woods started to sparkle with clear, yellow sunlight.

She approached Lavender Lane just as Sonny was mid-tumble.

"Tra-la-la-la ..." she sang to herself.

Suddenly, up ahead, she saw little Sonny tumbling down from the treetop, as if in slow motion.

"Oh no!" she cried.

All the little animals looked on in horror as Sonny fell. They scrambled around, trying to figure out the best spot to catch him.

But before Sonny reached the ground, he hit a springy branch and bounced off it . . .

Bounce!

Then sprang back upward into the tree . . .

Boing!

Ending up right inside the nest of a mother bird and her five babies with a

bump-thud!

The baby birds all went squawk!

They made a lot of noise because they had no idea what had hit them. It's not every day that a squirrel ends up in the middle of a bird's nest!

Duchess Tulip couldn't quite believe her eyes.

The babies flapped into a panic! A mass
of fluffy feathers exploded as the five little
birds tried to fly away from Sonny, even
though their wings were not strong enough.

Duchess Tulip didn't know who to help first! She lay down her gifts, getting ready for action.

"I'm going to need as much help as possible with this problem!" she said as the birds half-flew and half-ran away from their nest, along branches of the big tree.

Duchess Tulip rang the bells for the Superfairies. Then she flew up to the nest, speaking gently to Sonny and the birds.

"Hey, let's get this little squirrel out of there so you can have some peace, OK?" she said.

Sonny nodded gratefully, as did the mother bird, who was desperately trying to round her chicks back together.

Duchess Tulip carried poor, confused Sonny down to the woodland floor. He was very unsteady on his feet — his head was still spinning from the fall.

"Lie down by this tree," said Duchess Tulip, "and take nice calm breaths."

Susie and Martha came racing over to look after him.

"Oh, Sonny!" said Susie, hugging her brother. "I'm so glad you are OK. I feel terrible for letting this happen!"

"I'm OK," said Sonny, clinging to his big sister. "But I'd like to see Mommy and Daddy!"

Basil and Billy looked very sorry indeed.

"I feel so bad!" said Basil.

"Me too!" said Billy. "We should never have let him go way up the tree. He was trying to impress us!"

Basil nodded. "We should have said 'Good job!' for jumping off the log. That was enough for a little squirrel to do!"

"You are right, boys," said Duchess Tulip. "Luckily, he's OK. You should have taken care of Sonny. Do you promise nothing like this will happen again?"

Basil and Billy nodded.

"I think you mean it. Now, run off and play nicely in the sunshine. I still have work to do here."

Duchess Tulip went to help round up the baby birds.

"Come on, little ones," Duchess Tulip said softly. "I will take you back to your nest."

But they were scared and hid stubbornly in tiny holes dotted all over the tree.

"Oh dear!" said their mother. "They won't come out!"

Chapter 4

Superfairies Help Out

There was a cheer from the animals as the Superfairies' fairycopter landed.

Rose, Berry, Silk, and Star flew to the oak tree.

"Hello, Duchess Tulip!" they cried.

"Hello, Superfairies!" replied Duchess Tulip. "Things have gone wrong here. Poor Sonny needs some loving care, and the baby birds are too nervous to come out of hiding."

Rose went straight to see Sonny, blowing him healing kisses.

"Oh, I'm feeling better already!" he said.

Soon he felt well enough for Susie to take him home.

"Now let's think about what we should do for the birds," said Duchess Tulip.

"I could search for the birds with my super eyesight," offered Berry.

"A good plan — that will be part of what we need to do. But it doesn't help get them out of their hiding holes," said Duchess Tulip.

"I could make some Rescue Silk for them to climb along," suggested Silk.

"True. And that's a great idea. But they are so tiny, they could fall through the gaps," said Duchess Tulip.

"Maybe I could dazzle them," volunteered Star.

"A nice idea. But it might startle them rather than tempt them out," said Duchess Tulip.

"What about my healing kisses?" said Rose.

"Lovely, but only once we've gotten them safely back in the nest," advised Duchess Tulip.

Rose nodded. "I agree. There has to be something that would tempt them out of hiding. That's what we need to think about."

"Oh, please help me get them back," said the mother bird. She was getting very impatient to have all her family back together. "They will be hungry. I was just about to go out looking for food when Sonny landed in the middle of us!"

"Don't worry — we'll rescue them," said Rose. "We always do. We have to think of what's best — not what's quickest!"

Duchess Tulip flew around in a circle while she thought about what to do.

"I have an idea!" she said. "Superfairies, let's have a team chat. Come and join me!"

The Superfairies gathered around the duchess to hear the plan.

"Let's each take a piece of this tasty bread and see if it can tempt them out of hiding. Their mother said that they are hungry. Food could be just the thing!"

"Great idea, Duchess Tulip!" said Rose.

The Superfairies and Duchess Tulip circled the tree, whispering to the baby birds and offering the scrumptious-smelling bread.

"Don't be afraid!" said Duchess Tulip.

At first, there was no response.

Then one little bird poked its head out of its hiding place.

"Peekaboo!" said Rose.

"Oh, hello!" said Star.

And the other little birds soon appeared too!

"Hey, little bird!" said Silk.

"I bet you're hungry!" said Berry.

At last, all the birds were back with their mother.

"Oh, thank you!" cried the mother bird as her babies followed her into the nest. They feasted on even more of the delicious bread.

Rose blew healing kisses to the birds.

"Well, I think it's time we had a snack and caught up on other news!" said Duchess Tulip, feeling satisfied that everyone was OK now.

"That sounds like a lovely idea!" said Rose.

"Why don't you come in the fairycopter over to the cherry blossom tree?" said Superfairy Star. "We can have some rosehip honeybuns and elderflower tea."

"That sounds just great," said Duchess Tulip, flying to the fairycopter with the four Superfairies.

It was time for some springtime fairy fun back at the cherry blossom tree.

After a delicious snack and lots of chatting, the Superfairies and Duchess Tulip danced around the maypole. And as they did, the animals of Peaseblossom Woods came to join them.

It was time to celebrate the new life of springtime, and everyone wanted to dance with Duchess Tulip to welcome in the season. Basil Bear and Billy Badger took especially good care of Sonny Squirrel at the party.

They danced and sang until dark, then fell asleep under the spring stars.

SuperFairies

Farrah the Shy Fawn

Table of Contents

Chapter 1

Petals in the Woods

It was sunny and hot in Peaseblossom Woods.

Butterflies fluttered through the bright blue cornflowers and red poppies while the four Superfairies got ready to leave the cherry blossom tree.

"It's such fun wearing fresh flowers in our hair!" said Star.

"You look lovely!" said Rose with a smile. "But we must get going! I have the petals we collected yesterday here. Now, let's go scatter them!"

"Coming, Rose!" called Berry and Silk.

They flew out of the cherry blossom tree, up into the air and above the treetops. They began scattering flower petals on the path in the woodland below.

The petals floated down slowly, like perfumed pink raindrops. The air began to smell of petal perfume.

Farrah the Fawn was stepping through the woods daintily.

"Oh, what a lovely smell of flowers," she said.

Farrah saw the Superfairies at work.

"Hi, Farrah!" called Rose.

Farrah blushed shyly. "Hey, Superfairies, why are you scattering petals?" she called.

"We are marking the route for the Petal Parade," said Rose. "It will take place later today. Didn't you know? It always happens at the start of summer. The Petal Princess is coming!"

"Ooh, I forgot about the parade. I'm so excited," said Farrah.

"Well, we must keep on scattering," said Berry. "Goodbye, Farrah! See you later!"

"Bye!" called Farrah.

Farrah felt a little lonely now that the Superfairies had left. She went to tell her friend, Susie Squirrel, about the Petal Parade.

Susie *had* remembered about the Petal Parade. She was busy getting ready.

Farrah thought Susie looked lovely!

"Oh, your eyes look so sparkly," said Farrah.

"Thanks. I washed them with cucumber juice," explained Susie. "It brightens up tired eyes. Mom said so."

"Oh, and your cheeks are very rosy today!" said Farrah.

"I washed my face in the early morning dew," said Susie. "Granny said that was a good idea."

"Your fur is so shiny!" said Farrah.

"Ah, that's because I washed in rose water," said Susie. "Sorry I can't chat. I must polish my teeth with mint leaves. See you at the parade! Isn't it about time for you to get ready, Farrah?"

"Um, yes, I should, actually," agreed Farrah. But she had no idea what she was going to do to get ready.

Farrah's mom always said, "You are lovely just as you are." She didn't think beauty potions and perfumes were a good idea at all.

Mom will never let me try all that stuff. I'll never be as pretty as Susie, thought Farrah. *I wish I could look really beautiful for the parade!*

Farrah arrived back at her house. Mom was taking a nap.

Farrah had an idea.

I'll get ready all by myself and surprise Mom!

Farrah tried to remember all the things that Susie had used to make herself so sparkly and pretty.

Farrah decided to mix her very own beauty potion to make her look prettier.

She went into the kitchen.

First, she filled
a bowl with fresh
raspberry juice. Oooh,
juicy!

Farrah licked her hooves.

Next, she added lots of
honey. Oooh, sticky!

She took a little taste.
Yum!

Next, she poured in
sweet peach juice.
Oooh, messy!

Finally, she
added a handful
of oats and water.
Oooh, gloopy!

Farrah stirred the mixture together with a twig and then spread it over her cheeks and legs.

At first it felt warm. Then it felt tight. Next, it was a little itchy. And then it became horribly itchy!

"Ughhhh!" she cried as the mixture dried on her coat in sticky lumps.

"I'll need to go and wash this off in the pond. I don't think this is going to make me look pretty at all!"

Chapter 2

The Rainbow Plant

The pond wasn't far away. Mr. Frog was perched on his favorite lily pad.

"Hello, Mr. Frog!" called Farrah, jumping into the water.

"Hello, little one. Are you feeling the heat?" asked Mr. Frog.

"Yes, it's very hot, but I'm also itchy, actually," said Farrah.

As she splashed the mixture off her coat with the cool, fresh water, Farrah saw her reflection in the pond and sighed sadly.

"What's the matter?" asked Mr. Frog.

"Oh, it's just that I want to be pretty for the parade," she said. "Can you help me?"

"Well, I think you're already lovely, just as nature made you," said Mr. Frog. "But if you want to try a beauty treatment, why not use the leaves from the Rainbow Plant?"

"What's that?" asked Farrah.

"I've heard it's a plant that grows higher up on Rainshine Hill," said Mr. Frog. "They say one flower head has petals of every color of the rainbow. Apparently, it can make you beautiful! But I don't know if it's true . . ."

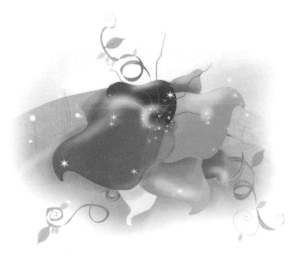

"I'll try it!" said Farrah. "That sounds like a great idea. The Rainbow Plant! It even sounds pretty!"

"Just follow the river upstream, and you will see Rainshine Hill. I believe the Rainbow Plant is about halfway up there."

"Thanks, Mr. Frog. I'll see you at the Petal Parade later on."

Off Farrah went in search of the Rainbow Plant.

She skipped along the riverbank . . .

. . . did cartwheels through Buttercup Meadow . . .

. . . cantered past Orlando Owl's house . . .

. . . and danced right up Rainshine Hill to the Rainbow Plant!

"Phew, I'm so hot!" said Farrah.

The petals were like the smoothest silk — and just as Mr. Frog had said, they were every color of the rainbow.

Farrah took some of the petals and began to rub them on her cheeks and legs.

Oh, please make me as pretty as Susie, she thought.

Farrah was exhausted after finding the plant. She decided to lie down in the sunshine for a few minutes.

Back at the cherry blossom tree, the Superfairies finished laying out the picnic blankets. They were for the party that would take place after the Petal Parade.

Wildflowers grew around the tree and large bowls of strawberries were placed on the blankets. There were jugs of freshly made lemonade and honey loaves too.

"Time to make petal crowns for our friends for the parade!" announced Rose, carrying a basket of freshly picked wildflowers.

The Superfairies gathered around and chose blooms from the basket. They got busy making the crowns.

Just as Rose was about to place her crown on her head, the Superfairies heard the bells ringing. Softly at first. Then stronger.

They got louder and louder.

Ting-aling-aling . . .

Ting-aling-aling . . .

The Superfairies forgot all about their flower crowns. The safety of the animals was the most important thing to them.

"Oh dear!" said Berry. "Someone's in trouble!"

"Prepare to rescue!" said Rose.

"Who's in danger?" asked Silk.

Rose checked the Strawberry computer.

"It's little Farrah the Fawn!"

"Where is she?" asked Berry.

"She's near Orlando Owl's house, not far from Rainshine Hill," said Rose.

"What's happened to her?" asked Silk.

"I can't see exactly. But she's not walking well, and she looks tired, dizzy, and confused," said Rose. "Orlando Owl rang the bells as soon as he saw her."

"Oh, poor little Farrah," said Star. "I wonder what the problem could be. Let's get to her as quickly as we can!"

The Superfairies jumped into the fairycopter and went through their rescue checklist as quickly as possible.

"Everything's in order," said Berry.

She always flew the fairycopter because of her super eyesight. She looked up ahead as she planned her route. "We'll follow the riverbank from above."

"Prepare to rescue!" said Rose. "5, 4, 3, 2, 1...go, go, go!"

The Superfairies flew over the woods in their fairycopter with Berry at the controls.

Chapter 3

Farrah in Trouble

Farrah made her way shakily down the side of Rainshine Hill. Orlando Owl flew overhead, feeling very worried about her.

"Are you OK, Farrah?" he asked. "I rang the bells for the Superfairies."

"Oh dear," she said. "What's happened to me? I don't feel well at all."

"What have you been doing?" said Orlando. "Can you think of anything that might have made you feel sick? Why are you so far out of the woods?"

Farrah thought that the leaves of the Rainbow Plant might have made her feel miserable. She wanted to explain everything to Orlando Owl, who was always helpful and sensible. But she couldn't get the words out right. Farrah was all mixed up!

"Rainbow leaves from the Rainbow Plant . . . Mr. Frog . . . Petal Parade . . . Susie so pretty . . . need the Superfairies," she chattered on, making no sense at all.

Oh dear, poor little thing. She thinks there's something called a Rainbow Plant! thought Orlando.

Farrah was so dizzy that she had to rest against a tree.

Berry and the other Superfairies were up above in the fairycopter.

On the woodland floor below, they could see Farrah's mom looking around anxiously. She had obviously realized that Farrah was missing.

"Thank goodness she seems to be heading in the right direction," said Rose. "We can let her know what's happening as soon as we land."

"I'm looking for a space to land," said Berry. "Does the Strawberry say where Farrah is now?"

Rose checked the computer.

"She was resting by a tree at the bottom of Rainshine Hill, but she's staggering back into the woods now. Near Orlando Owl's house," explained Rose.

"OK, I'll get as near to Orlando's house as possible," said Berry.

"Let's get everything ready," said Rose. "I don't know why she's so dizzy. She needs us right away."

Orlando Owl tried to tell Farrah to settle in one spot until the Superfairies arrived, but she wouldn't listen to his advice.

Farrah saw some beautiful scented flowers growing behind a cluster of trees.

"I can hear a stream. I'm so thirsty," she said.

Orlando followed, feeling worried that the Superfairies would never find them now.

Farrah walked through the cluster of trees and saw an archway of summer flowers up ahead. The sound of water was louder and stronger.

It looked as if the archway of flowers led to a secret place . . .

Farrah was curious.

Orlando Owl fluttered above her, looking over his shoulder to see if the Superfairies were there yet.

Farrah stepped closer to the flowery arch.

She could see petals floating in the summer breeze. She could smell sweet perfume. She could hear the tinkling water.

Hop!

Before she knew it, Farrah was on the other side of the archway.

She saw a fabulous, flowery fairy glade, with a stream of pure, clear water running through the middle.

What was this beautiful place?

The home of the Petal Princess! At the center was a fairy throne, and all around were flowers, birds, butterflies, bumblebees, and curious enchanted trees.

"Wow!" said Farrah.

She trotted farther into the flowery den.

Chapter 4

The Petal Parade

Farrah followed a path to the stream and noticed the Petal Princess looking at herself in the water. The princess was quite unaware that she had visitors — Farrah the Fawn and Orlando Owl were so quiet.

"A few flowers in my hair will look nice for the parade," said the princess.

She suddenly noticed Farrah.

"Oh, hello, little fawn," the Petal Princess said. "Are you all right?"

"Um, no, I'm not, actually," said Farrah.

"What happened?" asked the Petal Princess kindly.

"I don't know exactly. I was trying to look pretty for the parade this afternoon," said Farrah. "And I heard about the Rainbow Plant . . . May I have a drink of water?"

"Of course," said the Petal Princess. "This is all very confusing!"

"I rang the bell for the Superfairies," said Orlando. "I've been following her since I noticed her staggering down the hill. But I'm afraid to say she's making no sense at all."

Farrah drank from the clear, cool stream.

"I needed that," she said.

And with that, she fell to the floor as if she were fast asleep.

"Poor little thing!" said the Princess. "The Rainbow Plant does no good at all. It's a silly myth."

"You mean the leaves *don't* make you beautiful?" said Orlando.

"No, nothing can make you beautiful except the goodness in your own heart," explained the Petal Princess.

Just then, there was a fluttering of wings.

The Superfairies arrived at the woodland home of the Petal Princess.

"Hello, Petal Princess!" they cried.

"Oh, thank goodness!" said the princess. "How did you know to come here?"

"Our Strawberry computer led us here," said Rose.

"Just in time!" said the Petal Princess. "Farrah is very sick indeed."

"Let's look at you, Farrah," said Rose, examining the little fawn, who was still half asleep. "Poor little deer. Berry has gone to get her mom — they've been searching for her in the woods."

"She's had a drink of water," said the Petal Princess. "Whatever can be wrong?"

Rose examined Farrah for a few moments.

"It's most probably sunstroke!" said Rose. "Farrah has been out in the hot sun for too long."

"Rose, you are brilliant," said Star. "I'd never have thought of that. What should we give her?"

"Ah, lots of water, rest, and some healing kisses will do the trick!"

Rose blew gentle kisses onto Farrah's hot little forehead.

"Oh, that's better already!" Farrah said with a smile, waking up from her sleep. At that moment, her mom arrived with Berry.

Farrah nuzzled her mother happily!

"Now," said Star. "How can we keep Farrah out of the strong sun at the parade?"

"I think I can help with that!" said the Petal Princess.

She went away for a few moments and came back with a petal parasol for Farrah.

"I will hold you in my arms as I fly through the woods during the parade. This parasol will shield us both from the sun," said the Petal Princess.

Farrah beamed with pride.

"Thank you!" she exclaimed. "I can't believe it. Susie will be so excited for me!"

Later that afternoon, Farrah overcame her shyness as she flew at the head of the Petal Parade. She was delighted to be with the Petal Princess and the Superfairies.

"Hey, you look lovely!" called Susie.

"And so do you!" called Farrah.

Farrah had never felt so happy and proud.

It was time for the picnic back at the cherry blossom tree.

As the older animals enjoyed the delicious strawberries, the Petal Princess played games with the little animals.

"Let's play In and Out the Dusting Bluebells!" said Farrah, full of energy again.

"Thank you for taking care of her, Superfairies. You saved her life!" said Farrah's mom.

"Orlando Owl and the Petal Princess did that," said Rose with a smile.

The Superfairies were relieved that everyone in the woods was safe and happy again.

SuperFairies

The Copper Queen

Table of Contents

Chapter 1

Falling Leaves

The leaves on the trees in Peaseblossom Woods turned slowly from deepest green to shimmering shades of gold, bronze, and copper.

At first, one or two leaves dropped from the branches and floated through the woods to the ground below.

Then a handful of leaves fell.

Soon more followed.

After that, all the autumn leaves began to flutter down from the trees.

Fall . . .
Falling . . .
Fallen.

The branches became bare, and a
crisp blanket of golden leaves carpeted the
woodland floor.

Inside the cherry blossom tree, the
Superfairies were getting ready for the
arrival of fall and the Copper Queen.

"Not long until the Copper Queen's Masked Dance through the woods!" said Superfairy Berry. "Let's make our masks today!"

"I love the Masked Dance!" said Star. "It's so thrilling to see the beautiful Copper Queen, and dressing up is so much fun. Not to mention the dancing! You all know I love to dance."

Star did a twirl, but then, for a moment, she lost her smile. "But, why must the trees lose all the pretty leaves?" she asked.

"It's getting too cold and windy for them now," said Rose. "And the trees need to prepare for the big winter sleep so that they can burst to life again next spring! We can't expect them to go on and on, bearing leaves and blossoms and berries without a rest, now can we?"

"I guess that's true," said Star.

"Plus it's so fun to crunch in the leaves in the fall!" Berry added. "And there are always dress-up parties this time of year. And festivals and feasts too. I love it!

"Crunching through leaves is super fun!" Star agreed, brightening up a little.

"Think of it this way," said Rose. "Every season is so beautiful because it's unique.

They're all part of a perfect pattern for the whole year. There are so many delicious berries and fruits ripening now. We can make some jams to enjoy in winter!"

"And in spring, there are snowdrops and daffodils to admire!" said Silk.

"I love the warm sun and ripe strawberries in summer!" said Berry.

Star was happy with these thoughts and danced through to the kitchen to start

making some plum jam for the feast. They
would all be hungry after the Masked
Dance.

Out in the woods, the young animals
collected decorations for their masks.

"I can't wait to wear a mask at the
dance!" said Susie Squirrel. "And see the
Copper Queen for the first time."

"Me too!" agreed Martha Mouse.

They had heard all about the beautiful
Copper Queen and were excited to see
her. It would be such fun playing hide-and-
go-seek behind their masks at the dance!

"It's as if the whole world has turned
to gold!" squealed Violet the Velvet Rabbit.
"Granny told me this would happen, but
I've never seen it before! Everything is so

beautiful! I've even found some gold leaves for my mask."

"And I've found some cool sycamore helicopters!" Susie Squirrel said.

"Look! These pretty feathers will look great on my mask. Ooh, they're tickly." Dancer the Wild Pony giggled.

"Wow! I love these blackberry lilies!" exclaimed Cloud, Dancer's sister. "We're going to look so lovely!"

Basil Bear, Sonny Squirrel, and Billy Badger had already finished making their masks. They wanted to play now. They moved to a wider part of the woods, near the meadow.

Basil had made a ball by rolling grasses and moss tightly together.

"OK, you can be in goal, Billy!" shouted Basil. "And, Sonny, I'll be the striker. You pass the ball to me. Got that?"

At first, Billy and Sonny did as they were told.

"This way!" called Basil.

"Pass to me!" Basil yelled.

"Faster!" shouted Basil.

"My ball!" Basil insisted.

"That was a goal!" Basil complained.

Basil chased after the ball as it rolled toward the river. Billy and Sonny huddled together.

"Is it just me, or is Basil being super bossy today?" said Billy.

"It's not just you. I think that too!" agreed Sonny.

The boys tried to make the game more equal. They called out some instructions to Basil.

"Basil, you pass it to me!" called Sonny.

"Yeah, this way!" said Billy. "And it's your turn to be goalie."

Basil ignored his friends. As far as he was concerned, it was his ball, his rules.

Finally, Billy snapped.

"Stop bossing us around, Basil. This isn't fun!" said Billy.

"Yeah," agreed Sonny. "You're way too bossy. We want to get a turn with the ball. You're not being fair to us! It's not all about you."

"It's not about taking turns," said Basil. "It's about who is best!"

"Best at giving orders!" said Sonny.

"If you're going to be spoilsports, I'll take my ball and play somewhere else!" said Basil, sounding huffy.

Picking up the ball, he set off on his own. "Good luck without a ball!" Basil called over his shoulder.

Once Basil was out of sight, Billy turned
to Sonny.

"Oooh, Basil is sooo
annoying. Let's play
a trick on him!"
he said.

Sonny
thought for
a moment,
trying to
imagine what
some of his
bigger cousins
might do. "Let's
hide from him, then
call his name!"

"Hee-hee," laughed Billy gleefully.
"Great idea!"

Sonny looked around. "We should both
hide in different places. Then we'll call

and whistle at the same time. Basil won't be able to figure out which direction it's coming from."

"Good thinking," said Billy. "I'll go behind this mound of earth over here . . ."

"And I'll climb that tree over there," said Sonny. "Try not to laugh when he gets close!"

"You're right!" agreed Billy. "That'll give it away. Do you think Basil will come back this way soon?"

"Well, he has to pass here to get home," said Sonny. "And he really hates playing on his own . . ."

"Yes, because he doesn't like not having someone to boss around!" agreed Billy.

Chapter 2

Hide-and-Go-Seek

The boys got into their hiding places. Billy crouched down low behind the mound. Sonny lay flat on his stomach on a wide branch.

Then they waited.

Basil kicked the ball here and there near the Mousey House. At first, he enjoyed playing on his own. But after a while, he became bored. He decided to head back to the spot where he'd left his friends.

Basil wandered back through the woods, whistling to himself and singing rhymes. Then he heard his name being called.

"Basil!" called Sonny from the tree branch.

"Basil! Where are you? We'd really like to play with you again!" called Billy from behind the mound.

Basil was glad to hear his friends' familiar voices, but he couldn't figure out where they were coming from.

He looked to the left and the right. He looked in front and behind. He checked above and below. But he couldn't see his friends anywhere.

Sonny called again. "Basil!"

"Hey, where are you?" replied Basil.

"Here!" said Sonny, not giving away any information to help Basil.

"We're over here," Billy added. "Hurry up, we're having so much fun!"

"But I can't see you anywhere!"
Basil complained. He was getting very
frustrated.

A cold wind was starting to blow
through the woods. Basil spun around,
looking in every direction. He charged
along the pathway and suddenly . . .

FELL.

"Aaaarrrgh!" Basil screamed. "I'm f-a-l-l-i-n-g . . ."

He disappeared under some leaves.

Billy and Sonny peeked out from their hiding spots, trying to see what was going on. What had happened to Basil?

Billy rushed over to where Basil had disappeared. "He's fallen down a hole!" he shouted.

"Oh no!" exclaimed Sonny. He quickly climbed down from the tree and joined Billy.

They expected Basil to climb angrily out of the hole.

But he did not.

A few moments passed. They peered down the dark hole.

"Basil? Are you OK?" called Sonny.

"We're here!" said Billy. "We'll help you!"

The boys felt bad about their friend falling. They prepared to lean into the hole to help him out.

Just at that moment, a fierce wind whipped through the woods.

Whoosh!

The wind was wild and strong. It picked up Sonny and Billy and carried them through the woods.

Leaves of copper, bronze, and gold

flapped
flew
tossed
and
swirled

in every direction.

When the angry wind finally settled, Sonny and Billy were nowhere near where they had started.

"We need to go back and help Basil!" said Sonny.

The boys went back as quickly as they could to help Basil. Eventually they arrived back at the wide part of the woods near the meadow. There were leaves everywhere. The hole Basil had fallen into was nowhere to be seen.

"Basil! Basil! Where are you?" cried Sonny.

There was no reply.

Sonny went to look behind all the big trees.

Billy went down to the river to look.

There was no sign of him.

"Oh dear," said Billy. "What if he's hurt in that hole, and now we can't find him?"

"We have to keep looking!" said Sonny. "You go that way. I'll go this way. Call his name! We can meet back here in a few minutes."

"OK, good idea," said Billy.

"Basil!"

"Oh, Basil!"

"Basil, where are you?"

"We're sorry, Basil!"

The boys tried their best, but they simply couldn't find Basil and were frantic with worry.

There was only one thing to do. Sonny and Billy rang the bells for the Superfairies.

Ting-a-ling-a-ling!

Chapter 3

Time to Rescue

Over at the cherry blossom tree, the Superfairies heard the bells and sped into action.

"Forget the masks! The jam can wait! Let's get ready to rescue!" said Rose.

The Superfairies gathered all their rescue kits together, lifted their wands, and met in their fairycopter.

As Berry prepared for takeoff, Rose looked at the Strawberry computer to see what the problem was.

"I can see Sonny and Billy. They look frantic with worry near the meadow," said Rose. "But there's a split screen.

Basil looks like he's trapped in a dark hole somewhere!"

"This sounds very worrying!" said Berry. "I'll get us there as fast as I can! Five, four, three, two, one . . . go, go, go!"

The Superfairies were soon in the air. Before long, the fairycopter landed next to Sonny and Billy.

"Thank goodness!" said Billy when he spotted the Superfairies. "We were playing hide-and-go-seek. Basil fell in a big hole.

Then a big gust of wind whipped up all the leaves, and we were carried away. Now we can't find him. There are too many leaves for us to move them all."

"Oh dear," said Rose. "Have you tried calling his name?"

"Yes, and no reply!" said Billy sadly. "We've looked everywhere."

"Let's start by flying across the whole area, calling his name," suggested Star.

The Superfairies tried that, but Basil still did not respond.

"There must be something else . . ." said Berry. "I know! Let's see if the Strawberry computer's heat-search system can pinpoint where he is!"

"Good thinking," said Rose. She took out the computer and pressed the heat-search key.

The Strawberry started to flash, and the screen was filled with swirls. It began to beep.

Flash! Bang! Crash!

"Oh no! The Strawberry computer has crashed," said Rose.

"Oh, please think of something," Sonny begged. "I want to say sorry to Basil about hiding from him!"

"Who could help us to move these leaves?" said Rose.

The Superfairies all looked at each other. "The Copper Queen!" they said at once.

Rose quickly flew to the Copper Courtyard at the end of the woods. The other Superfairies waited anxiously. It seemed to take forever for Rose to return.

Finally Rose reappeared. This time, the magnificent Copper Queen was by her side!

The Copper Queen was exceptionally beautiful. She had long, flowing hair, a magnifcent gown and cloak, and a berry-leaf crown.

"The Copper Queen is going to dance all the leaves away from here. Then we should be able to see the hole," said Rose.

"Hurrah!" everyone cried.

"Thank you, Copper Queen," said Star.

The queen smiled but did not speak. She began to fly over the area where Basil was lost. Her movements grew faster and faster. As she danced in loops in the air, the leaves circled around her.

The Copper Queen moved behind the circles of leaves. With a great surge of power . . .

Puff! Whoosh! Shoo!

She blew them all away to another part of the woods.

The woodland floor was suddenly clear of leaves. In the middle of the clearing was the hole into which Basil had fallen.

"Thank you, Copper Queen!" said Rose. "Come on, Superfairies, there's no time to waste."

The Superfairies hovered over the hole. They could see Basil at the bottom, curled up in a ball.

"Basil, it's Rose," called the kind Superfairy.

Basil did not respond.

"Oh no!" cried Sonny. "Is he going to be OK?"

"Yes, I think so," said Rose. "But the fall might have hurt his head and made him sleepy. I will blow him my healing kisses."

"It's dark in there," said Star. "Let me use my magic and do a dazzle so you can see."

"Three, two, one, prepare to dazzle," said Star.

Twinkle! Dazzle! Sparkle! Ta-da!

"Much brighter!" said Rose. "Thank you, Star!"

Rose floated down next to Basil and knelt beside him, blowing kisses.

Slowly, Basil began to open his eyes. "Oh, my head aches. Where am I?" he asked.

"It's OK, Basil," said Rose. "You fell down a hole in the woods, but you're all right now."

Berry hovered the fairycopter overhead. Silk spun a rescue silk and fastened it around Basil. They raised him to the safety of the fairycopter.

Star fixed a bandage around Basil's head. With the feather cloak around his shoulders, he felt much better.

"Thanks to the Copper Queen!" said Rose.

The Copper Queen smiled shyly. "I'm always happy to help," she said.

Chapter 4

The Masked Dance

Later that day, the animals met the Superfairies by the cherry blossom tree. At last it was time for the Masked Dance!

Superfairy Rose looked pretty in a mask made from rose petals.

Superfairy Star looked shimmering in a mask made from gold leaves. Superfairy Berry wore a mask of rich, dark berries. Superfairy Silk's mask was fashioned from feathers.

The animals looked splendid too. They all wore beautiful masks, which made hide-and-go-seek very easy to play!

Susie, Martha, and Violet held hands as they danced, enjoying their pretty masks.

"No one will know who we are!" said Martha.

"But we know who you are!" said Sonny. "You can't hide from us."

Basil, Sonny, and Billy put on their masks too.

"We promise we won't play any tricks on you, Basil!" said Sonny.

"We'll never argue again," agreed Billy.

"I wasn't being fair," said Basil. "I should have shared with you. That's what friends do.

And I promise I won't boss you around again."

"Let's see how that goes!" Sonny said with a laugh. The three friends giggled and hugged.

A gentle wind whooshed through the woods at that moment.

"Here comes the Copper Queen!" called Susie, spotting the queen in the distance.

The Copper Queen blushed a little as everyone admired her. She didn't like to be the star.

"She's gorgeous!" gasped Martha.

The Copper Queen danced all the way through the woods, bringing down the last of the leaves as she went. The Superfairies and all the animals danced behind her in their fancy masks.

They stopped at a roaring bonfire —
Crackle, Spark, Careful —

to toast marshmallows —
Splodge, Goo, Yum!

After that, it was time for a full feast.
There was toasted nut-bread with butter
and plum jam. There were pumpkin pies,

warming soups, and yummy honey sponge pudding. There were delicious rhubarb and raspberry juices to wash it all down.

At the end of the Masked Dance, everyone was tired from dancing and had full tummies. Then they took turns singing songs.

"I don't want this to end!" said Susie Squirrel, even though it was way past her bedtime. She was exhausted from having so much fall fun.

"I know!" agreed Violet. "We live in the best place in the whole world. I love how every season is so different."

"But autumn is especially beautiful," said Martha.

With a little nod of her head toward the Superfairies, the Copper Queen left the woods. As she disappeared, an amazing display of fireworks lit up the sky.

The Superfairies danced around the bonfire with all the animals looking on.

It had been a magnificent Masked Dance, and everyone had gotten along so well.

No bossing around at all. No tricks. And no accidents.

Everything in Peaseblossom Woods was just fine.

SuperFairies

The Snow Fairy

Table of Contents

Chapter 1

Snowy Day

It was a snowy day in Peaseblossom Woods, and everyone was getting ready for the Snow Fairy's Sparkle Ball. The ball only came around once a year, but it was well worth the wait.

Lacy snowflakes tumbled from the sky and landed silently on the snowy ground. Icicles hung from tree branches like delicate crystal jewelry. Inside the cherry blossom tree, the Superfairies were admiring the pretty winter landscape.

"Everything looks so beautiful in a blizzard!" exclaimed Star, looking out of the window of the cozy living room.

"I love snowflakes. Is it true that every single one is different?"

"Yes!" said Berry. "That's true. But when they melt, they all turn to water just the same!"

"I don't want the snow to melt!" said Silk, twirling. "I wish it could be winter forever!"

"But wouldn't you miss the spring flowers?" Rose asked. "And the summer sun? And the autumn colors?"

"Maybe just a tiny bit," admitted Silk. "But isn't it lovely being all snuggled up in our sweet little house with the fire and lanterns and delicious food?"

"It definitely is!" said Rose. She fluttered over and warmed her hands in front of the crackling fire.

"I hope we can make it through all this snow to Icy Hollow for the Sparkle Ball," said Star.

"Me too!" said Berry. "I can't wait to see if the Snow Fairy likes the winter crown we've made for her this year." She attached some more berries and crystals to the wonderful, delicate crown she'd made. It dazzled on the dining table.

"That looks just beautiful!" Rose exclaimed. "Well done, Berry! I love it!"

"Thanks, but it isn't just my work," said Berry. "We've all worked hard on the crown. I think the Snow Fairy will love it too!"

"Let's try on our gowns for the ball now!" suggested Silk.

"Yipppee!" cried Star. "I just adore dressing up!"

"Remember we don't have long until we have to leave!" said Rose.

"Hurry then! I want to see how we look!" said Star.

In the woods, the snow was coming down. It covered the ground like thick frosting on a cake. It was almost too cold to play outdoors. Even so, the animals were very excited about the Sparkle Ball.

Over at Copperwood Stables, the ponies were almost ready to leave.

"It's time to gather everyone for the ball!" said Dancer the Wild Pony. "Are you ready, Cloud?"

"Yes! I just hope that our feet don't freeze in the deep snow!" Cloud replied.

"It's not too far," said Dancer. "If we run, we will hardly notice the cold. Let's go!"

Dancer and Cloud set off through the woods. They pulled a pretty painted caravan behind them to collect their woodland friends. They lifted their dainty feet through the thick snow, kicking up little flurries of soft snow as they went.

"Are your feet really cold?" Dancer asked.

"Not as bad as I feared. I'm just so excited!" said Cloud. "I can't wait!"

At the big oak tree, the rest of the animals waited in a huddle for Cloud and Dancer to arrive. Violet the Velvet Rabbit and Susie Squirrel couldn't stop chattering about what the Snow Fairy's gown would look like.

"I think it will be as white as fresh snow and very elegant!" said Violet.

"Maybe it will be embroidered with snowflake designs!" exclaimed Susie.

Sonny Squirrel and Basil the Bear Cub were also looking forward to the ball.

"I can't wait to slide along the icy dance floor," said Sonny.

"And chase each other!" Basil agreed.

Billy Badger and Martha Mouse were most excited for the feast. It was a famous feast, and the little animals had never been to it before. But they had heard all about it from older relatives.

"There will be warm herb bread with creamy butter and lots of fruit pies!" said Billy. "Yum!"

"I am hoping for iced fairy cakes,"
Martha said. "And piles of ginger-cream
cookies too! I love those!"

Just then, Dancer and Cloud arrived at
the big oak tree. The animals were thrilled
to see them. They piled into the caravan,
chattering and giggling as they did so.

The journey to Icy Hollow was hard
work for the dainty ponies. Thankfully,
with all the animals singing cheerful
winter songs, the time passed quickly.

They sang merrily:

"Crackling flames,

Winter games.

Toast your toes,

Warm your nose.

Hug your friend,

Warm cheer to send!"

"We're here!" cried Cloud as Icy
Hollow came into view. "At last!"

Chapter 2

Arrival at Icy Hollow

The animals hopped out of the caravan and looked around at Icy Hollow with wonder.

"It's dazzling!" said Susie.

"The icicles look like diamonds!" Martha exclaimed.

"It's an ice palace!" said Violet.

"Oooh, look! Here come the Superfairies in the Fairycopter!" said Martha. "I bet they'll look so beautiful."

The door of the Fairycopter burst open, and the Superfairies fluttered out. Rose carried the box holding the winter crown for the Snow Fairy.

"I hope the crown for the Snow Fairy is in that box! Is it true that it will light up if snow falls on it?" said Susie.

"Of course it won't!" tutted Sonny. "You say such silly things, Susie! Really!"

"We just saw the Snow Fairy!" Star called to the animals. "She's circling the sky above Icy Hollow to welcome us all."

Violet, Martha, and Susie held hands and looked to the sky with wonder.

"I can't wait to see her!" Violet exclaimed.

"There she is!" cried Susie. She gasped as the Snow Fairy came into view. "Oh, the gown is even lovelier than I imagined it would be."

The Snow Fairy floated down to join the animals, smiling widely to show pearly white teeth. Four snowy owls flapped around her as she flew, protecting her.

The Snow Fairy's white cloak was trimmed with fluffy down feathers, and she wore feather-lined boots of ivory velvet. Her golden hair fell in waves down her back, and her hair was covered with snowdrops. Her lips were of deepest red and her cheeks of palest pink, flushed by the cold air. On her hands she wore a warm velvet muff.

Once the Snow Fairy was seated on her throne, the snowy owls perched near her. Then the Sparkle Ball officially began!

Rose placed the crown in its box behind the throne. It would stay safely there until the ceremony to crown the Snow Fairy as Winter Queen.

The band struck up a tune. Dancer and Cloud danced with Violet and Susie.

But Sonny, Billy, and Basil didn't enjoy dancing.

"It's going to be *ages* until the feast," complained Billy. "What shall we do first?"

"My mom said I have to be really good," said Basil, "otherwise I'm not going to be allowed to go to any special events *ever* again!"

"Same here," said Sonny. "Dad said he'll be so embarrassed if I'm naughty! I have promised to be good."

Billy looked behind the throne at the box containing the Snow Fairy's crown. He lifted the lid. It seemed to be winking at him.

It dazzled!

It twinkled!

It sparkled!

"Sonny," Billy whispered, "should we take the crown outside for a moment?

We can find out if it really *does* light up
in the snow. . . ."

"Oh, that would be so fun! But we
shouldn't really take it, should we?"
said Sonny, thinking about his promise
to his dad.

"We're not going to take it, just *borrow*
it," said Billy. "We can put it back before
anyone notices. No one will even miss it.
Don't be boring! Don't you want to see
if it lights up?"

Sonny grinned. He thought it was a brilliant idea. He was very curious to see if the crown would light up. But he was very scared of being caught and getting into trouble.

Billy didn't wait for his friends to reply. He padded over to the box and lifted the crown from it. Before anyone could stop him, he ran out into the woods at top speed.

Sonny and Basil followed behind.

Outside, Billy held the crown up to the falling snow.

"Oh, wow! Look, it's lighting —"

But before Billy could finish what he was saying, a greedy magpie swooped down and . . .

SNATCH!

The bird grabbed the crown out of
Billy's hands and carried it up into the
snowy skies.

"Oh no!" said Billy. "What are we
going to do?"

"We must get the Superfairies to help
us!" said Basil. "Otherwise the Sparkle Ball
will be ruined!"

Chapter 3

Superfairies to the Rescue!

Inside the Sparkle Ball, the Superfairies heard bells ringing.

Ting-aling-aling!

"That's strange!" said Star to Rose. "We've never had to do a rescue at the ball before!"

"There must be a good reason if the bells are ringing," Rose replied.

Berry and Silk joined Star and Rose at once.

"Ready to rescue!" called Rose. All the Superfairies headed outside and huddled around the Strawberry computer, which Rose carried in her bag at all times.

"What can you see, Rose?" asked Silk.

"Billy, Basil, and Sonny are not far from here. There's a magpie too," said Rose. "Oh no! Look at the screen! The magpie has the Snow Fairy's crown! How could that have happened?"

The three boys joined the Superfairies. Billy was embarrassed.

"I'm really sorry," he said. "This is all my fault."

"What happened, Billy?" asked Rose. "How did the crown get outside?"

"We were just examining the crown for a minute," Billy said. "I wanted to see if it would light up. We were going to put it right back where we found it. But then the magpie flew down and took it right out of my hands."

"It was so quick!" Basil added, sounding flustered. "We didn't have time to do anything about it!"

"Did you see which way the magpie went?" asked Berry.

"That way!" said Sonny, pointing deep into the woods. The other two boys nodded in agreement.

"We must find the crown," said Rose anxiously. "Otherwise how can we crown the Snow Fairy as the Winter Queen?"

Billy felt very sorry and upset. Sonny and Basil were worried too — especially about what their moms and dads would say if they found out.

The Superfairies swooped into action, chasing after the naughty magpie.

"Come on," said Berry, using her bright eyes. "I can see the crown twinkling up ahead."

The magpie turned around and saw that he was being followed.

He picked up speed . . .

So the Superfairies flew faster . . .

And the magpie flew

Fast, Fast,
    FASTER STILL . . .

Then the tricky bird vanished into a big snowy tree.

"Where is he now, Berry?" called Star.

"He must be hiding inside the tree," said Berry.

The Superfairies flew toward the tree. There was a hole in the middle of it.

"Look!" whispered Berry. "Something is sparkling in that hole!"

"You're right, Berry!" whispered Rose. "Let's be very quiet and fly toward it."

"There he is!" said Berry. She could see the magpie hiding inside with the crown in his clutches.

"I will do a dazzle," said Star.

"And then I will zoom in to get the crown!" said Silk.

Star prepared to dazzle.

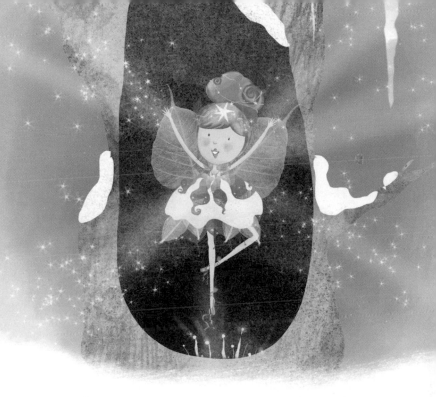

Twinkle!

Dazzle!

Sparkle!

But the magpie quickly flew out of the hole. He soared into the snowy sky again.

"After him!" cried Rose.

Chapter 4

Back to the Sparkle Ball

As the Superfairies zoomed after the bird, the Snow Fairy appeared beside them in the air.

"I heard the bells and followed you," she said. "I will make sure he cannot fly any farther."

With that, she waved her wand and created a gentle blizzard of snow. The swirling snow made it impossible for the magpie to see where he was going.

The naughty bird stopped on the nearest branch for safety. The crown fell from his clutches.

Berry swooped in to catch the crown.

"Phew! Got it!" she cried.

"Hurrah!" cried the other Superfairies.

"Well done, Berry!" said Rose.

The Snow Fairy and the Superfairies checked that the magpie was OK.

"I'm sorry," said the magpie. "I can't help taking shiny things. I just love them so much!"

"But if they don't belong to you, then you shouldn't take them," Rose told him gently.

"I know! I will try my best not to!" promised the magpie. Then he flew off to find his nest.

Billy, Sonny, and Basil were delighted to see the crown returned safely.

"Phew," said Billy. "Thank you so much! That was all my fault. I'm so glad it turned out OK!"

"Same here," said Basil. "I was scared it was gone forever!"

"I wasn't nervous," said Sonny. "I knew the Superfairies would find it!"

* * ❄ * *

Back at Icy Hollow, it was time for the crowning ceremony.

The band played a beautiful tune. A choir of animals sang to the Snow Fairy. She sat on her icy throne, shimmering with wisdom.

The music stopped as the Superfairies flew to the Snow Fairy.

"Are you ready and willing to be our Queen of Winter?" asked Rose.

"I am," said the Snow Fairy.

"Are you ready and willing to support us when we're in trouble?" asked Star.

"I am," said the Snow Fairy.

"Are you ready and willing to lead us toward spring?" asked Silk.

"I am," said the Snow Fairy.

"Are you ready and willing to celebrate the beauty of winter with us?" asked Berry.

"I am," said the Snow Fairy.

"Then," said Rose, placing the magnificent crown on the Snow Fairy's head, "I pronounce you the Queen of Winter!"

A huge cheer went up in Icy Hollow.

"Hush, everyone!" said Rose. "Let the new Winter Queen speak!"

"Thank you! Every one of you!" said the new Winter Queen. "After this party, I wish you all a beautiful sleep until spring! I will never let you down! And now, let's celebrate!"

"Hurrah!" cheered Billy, Sonny, and Basil. "All thanks to the Superfairies!"

"Let's do a line dance!" called Star, who loved to dance. "Come on, Dancer, help me!"

Susie and Violet followed the dance moves of Star and Dancer. Eventually the others joined in too, all holding hands.

"This is such fun!" said Susie. She could hardly dance as she was giggling so much.

"Billy, three steps *this* way!" called Martha. She gently pulled him in the right direction.

After the line dance, there was a waltz.

Finally, the Superfairies and the animals feasted together until everyone was exhausted. Then it was time for the Superfairies' song:

Fairies from the blossom tree,
Superskills galore have we.

Caring in this charming wood
For needy animals, as we should.

Twinkle, sparkle, dazzle, swish,
Tending animals as they wish.

And when a rescue's nicely done,
It's time to have some fairy fun.

Dancing, singing, twirling, glee,
All around our blossom tree!

Which Superfairy Are You?

1. What gift would you most like in winter?
   A)   a cozy scarf
   B)   a jar of cookies
   C)   a sparkly necklace
   D)   a storybook

2. What is your favorite game?
   A)   hopscotch
   B)   Mother May I ?
   C)   hide-and-go-seek
   D)   tag

3. Which is your least-favorite school subject?
   A)   art
   B)   English
   C)   math
   D)   gym

4. What color would you wear to a winter ball?
   A)   red
   B)   purple
   C)   gold
   D)   pink

5. If you had a winter wish, you would . . .
   A)   hold a worldwide party!
   B)   make jewelry from icicles.
   C)   dance in the snow.
   D)   heal everyone who is hurting.

6. You enjoy movies about . . .
   A)   adventures
   B)   animals
   C)   dancing
   D)   fairies

7. Your favorite tree is . . .
   A)   oak
   B)   fir
   C)   willow
   D)   cherry blossom

8. The treat you would make for a winter party is . . .
   A)   chocolate cake
   B)   apple pie
   C)   cheesecake
   D)   white-chocolate mousse

Mostly A — You are like Berry! You are helpful, sweet, and full of good ideas.

Mostly B — You are like Silk! You are exciting, brave, and adventurous.

Mostly C — You are like Star! You are cheerful, funny, dazzling, and bold.

Mostly D — You are like Rose! You are gentle, sensible, kind, and caring.

Superfairies
Fairy Cakes

It's not a party in Peaseblossom Woods without fairy food! Celebrate the seasons like the Superfairies and their friends with delicate, delicious fairy cakes. Fairy cakes, popular in the United Kingdom, are smaller than cupcakes and drizzled with icing, rather than covered with frosting.

What You Need

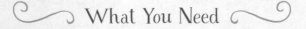

- ♥ 1 cup butter, softened at room temperature
- ♥ 1 cup sugar (superfine, if possible)
- ♥ 1 ¾ cup self-rising flour
- ♥ 4 eggs, beaten
- ♥ muffin pan
- ♥ 24 cupcake liners/baking cups

For icing:

- ♥ 2 cups powdered sugar
- ♥ 2–3 Tbs. warm water

What to Do

1. With a grown-up's help, preheat the oven to 355°F. While the oven heats, line your muffin pan with baking cups.
2. Beat butter and sugar together in a large bowl until light and fluffy. (Ask a grown-up to help you use an electric mixer.) Add half the flour and half the eggs and whisk until smooth.
3. Add remaining flour and eggs, and whisk until your batter is light and fluffy.
4. Spoon the batter into muffin cups and bake for 10–12 minutes, until the cakes are golden.
5. While your fairy cakes bake, mix up the icing, whisking sugar and water until smooth.
6. Once the cakes are cool, drizzle icing over the top and enjoy!

All About Fairies

The legend of fairies is as old as time. Fairy tales tell stories of fairy magic. According to legend, fairies are so small and delicate and fly so fast that they might actually be all around us, but are just very hard to see. Fairies, supposedly, only reveal themselves to believers.

Fairies often dance in circles at sunrise and sunset. They love to play in woodlands among wildflowers. If you sing gently to them, they may appear.

Here are some of the world's most famous fairies:

The Flower Fairies

Artist Cicely Mary Barker painted a range of pretty flower fairies and published eight volumes of flower fairy art from 1923. The link between fairies and flowers is very strong.

The Tooth Fairy

She visits us during the night to leave money when we lose our baby teeth. Although it is very hard to catch sight of her, children are always happy when she visits.

Fake Fairies

In 1917 cousins Elsie Wright and Frances Griffiths said they photographed fairies in their garden. They later admitted that most were fakes — but Frances claimed that one was genuine.

About the Author

Janey Louise Jones has been a published author for ten years. Her Princess Poppy series is an international bestselling brand, with books translated into ten languages, including Hebrew and Mandarin. Janey is a graduate of Edinburgh University and lives in Edinburgh, Scotland, with her three sons. She loves fairies, princesses, beaches, and woodlands.

About the Illustrator

Jennie Poh was born in England and grew up in Malaysia (in the jungle). At the age of ten she moved back to England and trained as a ballet dancer. She studied fine art at Surrey Institute of Art & Design as well as fashion illustration at Central Saint Martins. Jennie loves the countryside, animals, tea, and reading. She lives in Woking, England, with her husband and two wonderful daughters.

Visit our website at
www.mycapstone.com